The Time Stopper

A Mind Dimensions Story

Dima Zales

♠ Mozaika Publications ♠

This is a work of fiction. Names, characters, places, and incidents are either the product of the author's imagination or are used fictitiously, and any resemblance to actual persons, living or dead, business establishments, events, or locales is purely coincidental.

Published by Mozaika Publications, an imprint of Mozaika LLC.
www.mozaikallc.com

Cover by Najla Qamber Designs
www.najlaqamberdesigns.com

Edited by www.formatting4u.com and Mella Baxter

e-ISBN: 978-1-63142-041-2
Print ISBN: 978-1-63142-042-9

DESCRIPTION

I can stop time, but I can't change anything.

I can access memories, but not far enough.

My name is Mira, and my life is about finding the Russian mobster who killed my family.

CHAPTER ONE

"It's so smoky in here; it's like someone set off a bomb."

As soon as I say the stupid line, I Split into the Mind Dimension, and time seems to stop.

Victor is squatting over his chair, about to sit down. If this was still the real world, his legs would hurt in a minute or so. As it is, he's as aware of his muscles as a wax statue would be. Shkillet, a guy at the poker table, is frozen in mid-stare at my body—a position I often find men in. The other players are similarly stuck at what they were doing when I Split. The strangest thing in the room is probably the thick cigar smoke that's no longer moving. It looks eerie, like frozen clouds on an alien world. I don't smell the smoke now, which is a relief. I also don't hear anything other than the sound of my high heels clicking on the floor as I walk around the room.

I look at these men, these dangerous men, and an inner voice tells me, "Mira, no sane woman would voluntarily be here. Not even to merely observe this poker game, let alone play with these savages." It's funny how this inner voice usually sounds like my mom.

"You're dead, Mom," I mentally reply to the inner voice. "And I'm here to find the fucker who killed you. Can't we have an imaginary conversation without all this nagging?"

The inner voice sneers—but that's me. Mom was too nice to sneer.

The Mind Dimension makes it safe for me to walk around the room and peek at my opponents' cards without them being the wiser. When I'm in the Mind Dimension, everything stops in a single moment. No matter what I do here in this alternate world, when I get back to my real body—the body that's still sitting at the table—I'll still be in the same situation as I was before I Split: still being stared at by Shkillet, and still having just said that line about the bomb.

When I first learned I could Split, I was a little girl, and I thought my soul was leaving my body. But that was back when I believed in such things as souls, and God, and goodness—words that are meaningless to me now. Back in those days, I also believed in silly things, like the fact that there is a purpose to life.

I don't any longer. Not since that day.

Since that day, I haven't believed in anything but

myself. And sometimes—a lot of times—not even that. That little girl who believed in souls would certainly think I'm a stranger if she met me today.

And maybe, she would think I'm a monster.

Of course, that day did not just dispel my childish illusions. It also taught me more practical things, such as how impotent I am while in the Mind Dimension. How truly powerless. No matter how much I want to, I can't change anything in the real world. Like a ghost, I don't affect the world of the living. Maybe that's what I became that day—a ghost of my former self.

That day. Why does thinking about it always hurt the same way, no matter how much time passes? Why is it so vivid in my mind at a moment's notice?

For that matter, why does trying not to think about something bring that very thing into focus?

My mind flashes to that day as though I'm Reading other people, but it's as if I'm replaying my memories instead of someone else's.

I see myself walking home from school, my backpack heavy on my shoulders. I relive the excitement of seeing my dad's car in the driveway when I get home. He hasn't driven away yet, I think joyously, so I'll get a chance to say goodbye. That last line will be singed into my mind forever, but I don't know it yet.

And then I see the car explode.

I see it go up in flames.

I hear the most horrible sound.

Then . . . silence.

I open my eyes.

The fire is standing still.

The explosion had scared me so much that I automatically Split into the Mind Dimension, as sometimes happens under extreme stress.

Now in the Mind Dimension, I'm standing next to my other, frozen-in-time, self. She looks as terrified as I feel. I know that if I touch the exposed flesh on her/my body, I will leave the Mind Dimension—and the explosion will continue its destruction.

Leaving would've been a cowardly choice, a choice I didn't even think to make at the time. I would later regret that bravery—or rather, lack of imagination.

Instead of leaving the Mind Dimension, I run toward the car.

The flames are frozen. Unreal. As if they're made of red and yellow silk.

The full horror of the situation hits me only when I see the expression on Mom's face.

She looks white, or at least the parts of her face that aren't burned do. Her blue eyes are wide open, her irises almost black from her dilated pupils.

I open the car door and try to pull her out. In her body's rigid state, she's like a human-sized doll. As I'm straining under her weight, I know that this is futile. I've never been able to change anything in the real world by what I've done in the Mind Dimension. Still, I'm hoping that today will be different. That Mom will be out of the car in the real world simply because it matters so much to me.

Except the universe doesn't give a fuck what matters to me.

I quiet my mind and touch her face. I begin the Reading process, another brave action that will later haunt me. Like always, Reading her shows me the world through her eyes. I lose myself in her head. For that minute, *I* become *we*. The horror of my mom's last moments becomes mine—so it's me, too, who's beginning to realize we are about to burn alive.

Later, I will think about who caused the explosion and wonder if I can ever un-live it, but right now, I just leave her head and look into the car again.

Dad's face is free of burns. I will later hypothesize that the explosive was on the passenger side. His mouth is half-open in an expression of terror that contorts his whole face. I take all this in and am overcome with another idea that I will later regret.

I run to the side door and touch Dad's face through his open window, not really thinking about what I'm doing. Except I do know what I'm doing. I'm bringing him into the Mind Dimension. That's what touching another Reader does—and that's what Dad is, a Reader, like me and my brother.

Unlike Mom, who doesn't have our abilities.

As soon as I touch his skin, another Dad, a screaming Dad, shows up in the back of the car.

"Nyyyeeet!" He switches to Russian as he always does when he's stressed. Then he registers me and screams, "Mira, honey, no!" His accent is heavier than usual.

"It's okay, Dad," I soothe. "We're in the Mind Dimension."

"It's true. We are." He looks around, terror replaced with a different emotion on his face. A darker emotion that I can't exactly place. "Where is she?" he says after looking at the passenger's seat.

"I took her outside. I was hoping she'd stay outside."

Not saying anything, he gets out of the car and looks at Mom. "She's already burned."

"I know," I say thoughtlessly. "I Read her. She's in a lot of pain."

My dad looks like I flogged him with those words, but he quickly hides his reaction.

"In the real world, where are you standing, sweetie?" he says. "Tell me. Quickly."

"Over there . . ." I point. "Too far to help you."

"That's good." His shaking voice is filled with relief. "The blast shouldn't reach you there. But you still have to fall on the ground when you get back to your body and cover your ears for me. Promise me you'll do this. It's important."

"I promise, Dad." I'm beginning to understand what I have done to him. By pulling him out, I made sure that he could see himself dying in that car. That he could reflect on it. Dwell on it.

"I'm sorry." My voice also begins to shake. "I shouldn't have pulled you in."

"Don't say that." He smiles at me. It's one of the last smiles I'll have from him. "I'm glad I'll have a chance to . . . a chance to say good-bye."

I remember my thought right before I Split into the Mind Dimension and realize I had created something like an evil omen. A part of me knows that the idea is irrational, but I feel like I brought all of this on with that prophetic thought. *A chance to say goodbye.*

I squint as though I'm going to cry, but no tears come out.

"Don't." Dad reaches for me. "Let's spend the time we have left remembering the good times. Your Depth is only about a half hour—not enough time to spend on anything but happy memories."

He hugs me and tells me stories, determined to be with me for as long as I can stay, until I run out of Depth and become Inert—unable to go back into the Mind Dimension for a while. As I catch myself enjoying his stories and being with him, I hate myself more and more.

I'll later wonder what kind of bitch I was to extend such a moment for my father, but for now, I'm just happy to have him with me a little longer. For as long as I'm allowed.

"We're running out of time." Dad is trying his best to sound cheerful, but I know he's pretending. "You did the right thing," he says. "I'm really glad you pulled me out."

He's lying. Like my brother, Dad repeats lies to make them sound more convincing.

"To live even a few more minutes, to see you, is a treasure." His eyes look earnest, but I can see the truth. He isn't glad. He's terrified because he knows that as soon as my time runs out, he'll be taken out of the Mind Dimension and pulled back into his frozen body.

Into the explosion.

"There's nothing you can do for us now, Mira," he says. "Please take care of your brother; he's all you've got—"

I don't hear him finish that sentence because my time runs out. I will later grow to resent this limitation, my Depth. This finite amount of what-if time.

If only I could've stayed in the Mind Dimension forever. Then Dad and I could've talked forever. Or we could've explored that frozen-in-time world. Instead, I'm back in my body and the explosion is in my ears again, ears that feel like they might bleed. I fall on the ground, like I promised Dad I would. I welcome the pain of the fall because it numbs the pain from knowing that I don't have parents anymore.

With herculean effort, I pull my mind back to the present. To the poker table and the Russian thugs surrounding me. I really have to get it together. My Depth's being wasted as the seconds turn into minutes. If I run out of time, I'll be Inert for a while—which means no more Reading and having to play fair in this poker game, to boot.

I shake my head and try to focus, determined to forget Mom and Dad for the moment. I try to focus on something else.

Anything else.

To distract myself, I think of how strangely I experience emotions in the Mind Dimension. For example, if I cry there, because my face is dry once I get out, I don't feel as sad anymore. Sometimes things work the other way. I can be terrified when I get into the Mind Dimension, but once there, I'm much calmer. Probably because there I'm safe. So if I get any tears now, they would be gone when I'm back at that table. And tears should be falling down my face right now, but none come. Just like on that day. The worst one of my life—

I have to stop thinking about that day.

So I try to picture talking to my brother about emotions in and out of the Mind Dimension. He would want to study this phenomenon, as he—ever the scientist—would call it. It makes me feel somewhat better. Thinking of Eugene always helps take me out of the darkness, if only for a moment.

"I do take care of him. The poor bastard would've starved long ago without me, Dad." I'd say that to my father if I believed he was listening to me from Heaven. Of course, my father is not in Heaven or Hell—those are just constructs people make up to dull the pain of losing their loved ones. I know that, in reality, he's just gone, and nothing I say can reach him.

And that means I need to stop dwelling on what might've been and focus on the task at hand.

The fucker who put the explosive under my family's car might be in this very room right now.

I take a deep breath, finding comfort in anger and the violent fantasies of what I plan to do to him.

"It's time," I say out loud—though, of course, the frozen people can't hear it. "Let's see if any of you fuckers are thinking of explosions."

CHAPTER TWO

I'm hoping the guy I'm looking for, the guy who deals with bombs, will be primed by my words and think of setting up one specific explosion. I'll be the first to admit that this tactic is a long shot, but it's the only option I have since my Depth allows me to go back only a few minutes into their memories.

Not for the first time, I envy more powerful Readers. Those like the legendary Enlightened, the most powerful Readers of all, who have enough Depth to relive whole months, if not years, of someone's life. Someone like that would get the answer directly without any gimmicks, but I can't. There are no shortcuts for Readers like me. Given that Depth is spent at twice the speed when you Read, I have to be careful about running out of my measly half hour.

Whatever Depth I spend on Reading is going to be worth it in this case, though. Trying to learn the truth is why I come to these games. Well, that and the money from the wins—but there are better ways to make money gambling than coming here. Safer ways.

My strategy for today is to spend only seconds of my Depth on people I think as unlikely candidates, leaving extra time—even if it's just a few minutes—for the others.

One such unlikely candidate is Shkillet, the guy who's staring at me in the real world.

Shkillet is not his real name, but a street alias. Probably has something to do with his too-thin pasty-looking face. He resembles one of those skeletons we had in science class before I dropped out of school. The Russian word for skeleton sounds a lot like the word *skillet*, only with a *yet* sound at the end. Shkillet's lisp could be the reason for the *sh* sound at the beginning.

Or I could be completely wrong. I was pretty young when we left the Motherland, and I do get some of these little ethnic things confused now and then—which drives my brother nuts.

I look at Shkillet's cards. He's not holding anything I need to worry about. But he is staring at me—the real-world me. In fact, if I drew a line from his pupils to that me, it would land directly on her/my boobs. Boobs that are nicely displayed in my red strapless dress, thanks to the Victoria's Secret pushup bra.

I intended that effect, but I'm still annoyed. Fucking men.

Stepping around him, I take off his shirt.

I know it seems weird that I'd undress someone, especially someone this unattractive, but I do have a purpose. I'm looking for tattoos. Over the course of my investigation, I've learned that a man's tattoos in the Russian criminal underworld reveal a lot about him. Well, only for the ones who've been in Russian prisons, but those are the ones I'm looking for. The most dangerous. The ones without souls.

Those who'd plant bombs on innocent families.

Shkillet is what I call skinny-fat. His body is gaunt with his ribcage sticking out, but at the same time, his stomach is flabby. I don't care about his looks, though. All that matters is that he has no tattoos. He does have a large birthmark, however, that reminds me of a Rorschach inkblot test. A counselor showed it to me during the one and only time I tried therapy. Most of her inkblots reminded me of people's brains blowing up—understandable, given the reason I went to see her in the first place—but this guy's birthmark looks like an exploding heart.

Okay, so Shkillet either hadn't been to prison back home or nobody bothered to put any ink on him while he was there. Either way, he's not likely to be a high-status criminal and thus probably isn't the person I'm looking for. Therefore, he's good for a measly five-second jump into his head.

I put my hand on his neck as though trying to

measure his pulse. Where I touch people in the Mind Dimension never seems to matter, so I go for the least disgusting place. I clear my mind for Reading. The faster this part is, the more Depth I save. Eugene had figured out some techno-widgety new practice for me to improve how quickly I can do this, and I'm grateful for it with situations like this.

The feeling I get just before I'm about to Read someone comes over me, and I make sure I'm sent only a few moments back into his memories.

* * *

"It's so smoky in here; it's like someone set off a bomb," the girl says.

The sex bomb is talking about a real bomb, we think of replying, but decide against it. Not until we see how Victor responds. The guy's insane, and displeasing him is as easy as it is deadly.

This is why we realize that if we go through with our plan for the girl, we'll have to cut her throat afterwards. Had we just wanted to fuck her, then we could probably get away with leaving her alive afterwards—there are no rules against rape in this place. But we want her money, too, and that's why she'll have to die. Victor's underground casinos have only this one rule: retaliations due to game losses are forbidden. We shudder when we remember what had been done to the last guy who tried to pull some shit on a poker game winner. We'll have to ensure we're not caught.

We think about all the things we want to do to her before we kill her off, and get a painful hard-on. We imagine how we'd fill up that oh-so-fuckable pouty mouth of hers. We visualize grabbing those perfect titties, leaving marks, prying open those long legs . . . Our balls tighten in anticipation.

This is going to be even better than the last time. That whore from two days ago can't even begin to compare to this girl. Looks aside, that bitch hadn't even fought us, just meekly took it. The fight has become half the fun for us over the years. When they fight, and we finally bend them to our will, we feel the rush of power that's almost as fun as the sex itself. With this girl, it'll be even better because she's rumored to be feisty. The sarcastic remarks she's made throughout the game confirm it. So she'll likely fight, and fight well. We fantasize about her scratching our back with her perfectly manicured fingernails before we lock her wrists in a tight grip . . .

I, Mira, separate my own thinking from Shkillet's in horrified disgust. I need a shower. I need a dozen showers. I'm still in his head, but I can reflect on what I just learned without fully getting out. Separating my thinking this way allows me to spare my brain from getting more of the vile details of what he plans to do to me. Witnessing the memories of what he did to the poor girl he raped two days ago was terrible enough. And while I'm not clear if he killed her afterwards, I'm positive he's planning to kill me.

Given the circumstances, I dive a little deeper into his memories. I need to learn if he's armed and if there's anything else I need to know about.

We look at our cards. One fucking pair. Two more rounds like this, and we'll be completely broke. But not for long, we remind ourselves, feeling the weight of the ceramic knife in the holster in our boot.

It'll be best to do the deed swiftly. It has to happen here on the club premises before the bitch leaves and has the chance to get into her car.

Victor will be furious when they find the body. But he'd never suspect Shkillet. Getting no respect has some advantages—people underestimate us, and therefore, we can get away with anything.

I, Mira, separate again and think quickly. He managed to sneak a ceramic knife into this place. I guess the material didn't trigger the metal detector wands the bouncers pass over everyone's body upon entrance.

Damn it. This changes my strategy completely. I need to make sure to leave plenty of Depth to deal with this development. If one of these other men is the one I came here to find, it's his lucky day, because I'm skipping their vile heads.

Except Victor's. I've been waiting to meet him face-to-face for months because he's always seemed the most likely candidate, given what I've heard about him. There's no way I'm missing that chance now.

As I form a plan, I exit Shkillet's mind.

* * *

Still in the Mind Dimension, I approach Victor and unceremoniously rip the shirt from his body. As I do so, I note the pair of aces in front of him on the table.

And his tattoos.

Yeah, Victor's been in the Russian jail system—he's a *zek*, as these people call it. Russian tattoos fascinate me. Probably because Dad had one. He served time with a bunch of scientists for objecting to the nuclear arms race during the Cold War. His Reading skills saved his life, enabling him to get out of the prison camp after only a couple of months, but the hellish experience made him desperate to leave the Soviet Union. He waited years until he could, and by then, the Soviet Union was simply Russia. Still, as Dad liked to say about the new regime, "Nothing's changed—KGB still rules."

So now I try to memorize Victor's tattoos. I only recognize the meaning of the stars on his shoulders. *Vor v zakone.* Translated literally, it means 'a thief in law,' but the vernacular is a criminal authority of high caliber.

I examine him more. I've never seen this double-headed eagle tattoo before, though I think this is what the government symbol looked like back in the Czarist Russia. The Statue of Liberty super-imposed on the eagle also doesn't ring any bells. Perhaps Victor hates the Soviet Union and is reliving the pre-revolution glory days with this ink? Coupled with a symbol of America, maybe he's not so fond of communism, too? It's a theory that gains more credence when I realize that a lot of his prison images are anti-authority.

I also notice that Victor is ripped. How can I not? I am, after all, human. He's built like a swimmer, and his abs form a perfect six-pack.

Stop being a danger slut, Mira, I chide myself. *How can you even think about what he looks like after what was in Shkillet's head?*

Or, more importantly, given what I've heard about Victor. This tendency to drool over monsters is something I truly despise about myself.

So, to that end, I decide enough's enough. I need to give Victor a Reading and get the hell out. I'll be only half-empty of Depth, and that will have to be enough.

I put my arm on his chiseled chest, right on the serene face of Lady Liberty. Physical contact made, I concentrate.

I'm going back far enough to see what he did before he came into this room. With any luck, he might've been thinking of blowing up someone's car. If so, Shkillet won't be the only person I'll need to deal with . . .

* * *

We're inside Vera. She moans softly. With her bent over just the way we like, we have a nice view of her naked back. It's sinewy with muscle. In a perfect world, we like our woman to be a bit curvier, but there's something about her that we find attractive enough to overlook that fact. Our previous squeeze had nice love handles, but she, unfortunately, didn't appreciate our interest, instead opting to overdose while we were taking care of business. Women.

Besides the lack of curves on Vera, we also don't approve of the tattoo on her lower back. It's of Madonna holding the baby Jesus. When we fuck someone doggy-style, the last thing we need is a religious symbol staring us in the face, particularly since the tattoo artist made Madonna beautiful. Probably wanted to mess with the heads of everyone who'd ever fuck Vera in the future—which is a large number of people. Or, just as likely, the bitch arranged for the tattoo to have this effect herself.

As our thrusts deepen, she moans louder, and that brings us closer to the edge. In an effort to prolong the sensation, we direct our mind off the fucking and onto irrelevant things, like the dimples above her ass.

Unfortunately, they're actually a turn-on.

So then we try focusing on the little mole on her right shoulder blade. That works for a bit until we notice the way the sweat slicks her skin. Smooth, gleaming skin. Fuck. We lift our head to stare at the blank walls of the VIP room.

I, Mira, disassociate, albeit hesitantly. This is the first time I've ever caught a man fucking a woman, and it's . . . hot. It's nothing like Reading them while they fuck me. Of course, I'm not here on a hedonistic vacation. Each moment I spend watching this, a double moment is subtracted from my Depth—because that's how Reading works. Eugene explained that we share the time with the target. I guess that means that on some level, everyone can get into the Mind Dimension when touched, but non-Readers are pulled in only enough for us to Read them.

I fast-forward Victor's memories a few minutes into the future.

We're approaching the table and noticing the girl. She's the prodigy we've heard so much about, the only female *katala* we've ever met—though, to be fair, we met most of those card-shark shysters when doing our time in the all-male Gulag.

We look at her, this girl who's squeezed so many people dry at our establishment. She has the cheekbones and nose of Russian nobility. Someone in this girl's lineage must've survived the October Revolution back in 1917. Her features have a slight sharpness to them, along with an air of dignity. It's a contrast to the matreshka-like round face of someone like Vera, who looks like a common Russian farmer's daughter—and probably is.

With those big blue eyes, long eyelashes, and dark waves of hair, this girl reminds us of our daughter's latest pictures. Only Nadia looks much more innocent than this one, we think with a mixture of longing and pride. Keeping Nadia innocent is why we made the sacrifice of not being in her life all those years ago. She probably doesn't even know who we are, so there's no point dwelling on it. And even if she knows, she's in Russia, and we can't go back there.

"It's so smoky in here; it's like someone set off a bomb," the girl who reminds us of our daughter says.

That word—bomb—brings back flashbacks of that day in Chechnya when we lost two of our best comrades. Our heart rate increases, but then we calm down. The girl is just being a spoiled American princess. It happens to all the kids who arrive here. Her Majesty probably expected this illegal gambling club to enforce New York's non-smoking laws.

I, Mira, separate my mind from Victor's and feel a hint of disappointment. The fact that my words bring up his experience in Chechnya, which must've happened a long time ago, makes him unlikely to be the guy I'm looking for. Especially since he seems to have an aversion to explosions—almost a PTSD-type of reaction. It's not a certainty that he wasn't involved, of course, but it's enough for me to clear him. I'd crossed people off my list based on less credible evidence.

Thus decided, I exit his head.

* * *

I'm back in the silent room. I'm not going to Read the other players' minds. I'm going to conserve my Depth instead. I have two more things I have to do.

First, I take a look at the cards everyone else is holding. With the outcome of the next round in my head, I proceed to the second thing and run out of the room. Swiftly, I go through the dark corridor to the nearby bathroom. I check what I came here to check and confirm that it's still there—the thing that'll give me a chance when dealing with Shkillet. I'm a little calmer now and glad I took the time to explore this establishment in another Mind Dimension excursion; otherwise, I wouldn't have known about things hidden in nooks and crannies.

I run back to the room and approach my body. It's always strange seeing myself like that. Being able to examine myself from all angles used to magnify my teenage insecurities. Normal girls can drive themselves crazy with a mirror, but Readers have it much worse. I remember being depressed about the shape of the back of my ankles not long after my fifteenth birthday. Of course, since my parents' death, I haven't thought about shit like that ever again.

I prepare myself for exiting the Mind Dimension and reach out, placing my hand on my frozen self's face.

And just like that, I'm back in my body.

The sounds are back, and so is the smell of smoke. Victor completes the motion of sitting down in his chair. The dealer finishes dealing. Shkillet stops staring at me, and looks furtively at Victor to see if he would reply to my weird statement.

"What the fuck are you talking about?" says a bald guy who's smoking a cigar. "If someone brought a bomb in here, Victor would put that bomb into that yebanat's ass."

CHAPTER THREE

The next few rounds of poker proceed predictably, given that I know which cards everyone is holding, as well as the top cards of the deck. So obviously, I win every round I can. And as I win, I watch Victor's amusement grow. I'm not sure if it's my winning that he finds amusing or the men's reactions. They dare not give me any attitude, but when I sneak a look at Shkillet, I can tell he's barely hiding his anger. Today, out of spite, I've been winning more than I usually do, and two rounds ago, I called Shkillet's bluff—a bluff that would've probably worked if not for my Reading powers.

Since I don't have a lot of Depth left, I decide that now is the time for me to get out of here. Before I wear out my welcome, so to speak.

"Gentlemen." I stand up. "It's been a pleasure."

"Pleasure taking our money, you mean?" Victor, surprisingly, doesn't sound angry. More like he's teasing.

"Sure, that, and it's nice to finally put a face to the name . . . Victor." That might've come out too flirtatious, but hell, I'm too wired for finesse at the moment. As I start gathering my stuff, I see Shkillet begin to fidget. I can tell he's about to leave, too. He's determined to put that plan of his into motion.

I put my winnings into my purse and slowly walk out, trying not to look suspicious.

I know I should make a run for it once I'm in the hall instead of implementing my more dangerous idea of confronting him. But I don't. That would be like playing the last rounds of poker so Shkillet would win—something else I could've done, but didn't. He needs a lesson, and I'll enjoy giving it to him. Maybe with him, I'll finally get the chance to figure out if I'm capable of doing what must be done when the time comes. My brother doesn't think I'd take someone's life. He means it as a compliment, but that's not how I take it, and tonight, I'm betting my life that my brother is wrong.

I arrive at the bathroom door. Shkillet hasn't come out of the game room yet. I take out a pack of Marlboro Reds and a lighter from my purse. I don't really smoke, but pretending to smoke has come in handy at times. Being a girl with a cigarette in her hand is a good icebreaker when the room is full of men with lighters. So I'm a sort of social smoker, I guess. But unlike others, I hate every inhalation.

Sometimes when I smoke, I can almost feel the stuff making my lungs and teeth yellow and gross.

As I put the disgusting thing in my mouth, the game room door opens. I light up, inhale, and try not to cough while glancing at the door. Shkillet's there, and we make fleeting eye contact before I exhale the smoke.

Bait set, I walk into the bathroom.

I close the flimsy door lock behind me, hang my purse on a little hook in an effort to free my hands, and run to the toilet as quickly as possible given the slippery floor and my high heels.

The toilet lid is opened, and I catch a glimpse of the disgusting stuff in the bowl when I throw my now-useless cigarette into it. God, would it have been that difficult to flush the shit? The sight and stench of it reminds me of a nightmare I had a few times about a dirty bathroom. And this reality might be worse than that nightmare if I don't hurry up.

I reach for the water tank just as I hear the lock on the door being picked.

Shit. He's faster than I thought he'd be. He must've run down that hall like a maniac.

I frantically lift the heavy tank cover . . . just as the door lock fails.

"What the hell?" Shkillet says in Russian as he steps inside and sees me standing there with the lid in my hands.

Good. Not what he was expecting. And I capitalize on that by throwing the lid at his head with all my strength.

He's not fast enough to duck.

As he staggers backward with a grunt, I turn and grab the gun in the plastic zipped bag from the tank. I'd found this weapon in one of my earlier excursions in the Mind Dimension. I'm ripping the bag open when someone's hands grab my left arm.

It's Shkillet.

His fingers are like pincers digging into my flesh.

I Split into the Mind Dimension to assess the situation.

The sounds of his panting are gone, and I observe us from my new vantage point.

One of his hands is on my arm, and the other is reaching into his boot for the ceramic knife he's hiding there. His eyebrow is split open—must be where the lid hit him. The blood running from that wound makes his face look ghoulish.

I examine the bag in my hands. I've almost opened it, but I'm not sure if I'll make it before he gets the knife out and uses it. But I can do something else if I aim right.

I look at my statue-like face that's paralyzed in fear. I'll try my best to be calmer when I get back into my head. Calmer and lethal.

Grabbing my hand, I jump out of the Mind Dimension and desperately will my muscles to act. As though in slow motion, my leg kicks backwards, aiming for his shin. My foot connects with something.

"Bitch!" He falls to his knees. I must've hurt his

leg.

In the time I bought myself with the kick, I get the gun out. Whirling around, I see the knife already in his hand.

He swings, the knife swishing through the air an inch away from my leg.

Instinctively, I jump to the side, then slam the butt of the gun into his face. It connects with his nose with a disgusting crunch.

He looks stunned for a moment, and I do it again, swinging the heavy handle at his jaw this time.

He tries to grab me, so I hit the back of his head.

He crumples—his head landing right in that disgusting toilet.

Serves the fucker right. Now he'll drown.

I should gloat, but for some inexplicable reason, I get the urge to kick him away, to get his face out of that toilet. Do I actually want to save his life?

I take a closer look at him. His mouth and nose are above the water, so he won't drown in that muck.

Funny, but for someone who was just thinking of saving him, I feel a pang of disappointment. The practical side of me knows I can't let him live. So I take the gun safety off and aim the muzzle at the back of my would-be-rapist-and-murderer's head.

This is it.

Now I just have to pull the trigger.

Is my hand really shaking? What is wrong with me?

This man deserves to die. Maybe not as much as my parents' killer, but he does deserve it. And if I don't kill him, he'll likely come after me. So shooting him is self-defense. Or a pre-emptive strike, if I have to justify my actions.

And apparently I do—because I can't squeeze that trigger no matter how many reasons I come up with for doing so. Like: *he might be too chicken-shit to come after me.* Or: *this might be his first attempt at murder.* And even: *he might change his whole life around after this.* Yeah, right. I'm now grasping at straws to come up with excuses for myself, when the truth is that Eugene was right.

It's not easy to kill a person—even a bad person.

"Is someone in there?" someone says from the other side of the door.

Shit.

I rush to the door and open it a sliver.

"Hey there," I say to the guy at the door, who looks to be one of the bouncers. "I'm just powdering my nose, and I need to change after that. Can you please use the bathroom upstairs?"

The bouncer mumbles something derogatory about women but starts walking away. Taking no chances, I Split again and Read a second of the bouncer's mind. He's going upstairs—that's the good news. The bad news is that he's mentally cursing a specific woman, me, and not, say, women in general, or one of the few other possible women who visit this place, like Vera—Victor's fucktoy from the nearby VIP room.

I guess this makes my decision for me. I can't

shoot Shkillet now. The bouncer will know that I was the one who killed him, even if I run as soon as I fire the shot. I'm not keen to find out how Victor would react to my murdering someone in his place.

I could, though, hold Shkillet's head under the water until he drowns. That way, no one would come running right away, and I could get away. Plus, the bouncer wouldn't necessarily think I'd done it—I'm sure he's seen more than one drunk in Shkillet's position.

The big question is whether I can actually do it . . . since I wasn't able to pull the trigger.

Damn it. I hate that Eugene is right, and today isn't going to be the day I finally prove my worth to myself.

I stuff the gun into my purse and walk through the place, paranoid all the way to the exit that someone's going to notice the size of my purse. Luckily, no one stops me. It makes sense, since the time to distrust someone is when he or she is on the way in, not out. Plus, what male bouncer is going to be staring at my purse instead of my cleavage?

Still, I'm only able to breathe normally when I get into my car and put the gun into the glove compartment. Even though I don't need it, I didn't want to leave it for Shkillet in case he regains consciousness and decides to come after me. I might not be a cold-blooded killer, but that doesn't make me stupid.

The drive back home happens in a post-adrenaline-rush haze, for which I'm thankful. I don't want to think about what just happened. I just want to get home and unwind.

When I arrive at the apartment I share with Eugene, I take my high heels off and tiptoe into my room, stepping over all the junk in the living room. Not for the first time, I promise myself to tidy up, but obviously, not tonight. Closing my bedroom door, I'm super-grateful that I didn't wake my brother. My earlier plan for a dozen showers forgotten, I get into bed and pass out.

My sleep is interrupted by a recurring nightmare—a skeleton trying to strangle me.

CHAPTER FOUR

"Mira, is that you?"

My brother has this annoying habit of talking to me when my mouth is full or when, like now, I'm under a cascade of blissfully warm water, trying to relax.

"No, Eugene, it's some fucking stranger using our shower!" I slam the sliding door for emphasis.

"Thanks for saying the F word—now I know it's you!" He bangs on the bathroom door. "Come to the kitchen when you're done."

I wish I'd slept instead of tossing and turning all night. Still, the little sleep that I had should keep me going, and this shower is doing wonders.

I put on jeans and a T-shirt and head to the kitchen. My curiosity is piqued because I smell food—an oddity because I don't think anyone is here besides Eugene. Which would mean that, whatever dish the smell is coming from, he would've had to cook it.

"Happy birthday to you," my brother sings when I enter. "Happy birthday to you—"

"Eugene, please stop. My ears are going to wilt." I use humor to cover up the fact that I completely forgot about my birthday. With everything that's happened, it was the last thing on my mind.

"I made pancakes." He puts a plate in front of me when I sit down at the table. "Eighteen. One for each year."

"Is that what those brownish ovals are?" I give him a questioning look. "And isn't it supposed to be a candle for each year, not pancakes?"

"Aha!" He winks and brings his hands out from behind his back. He's holding a cupcake with a lit candle. The strawberry vanilla cupcake from the local Italian bakery that I like. It's a miracle he didn't burn his clothes standing like that.

"Thank you." I take the pastry and place it on the table. "And thanks for wearing a clean lab coat on this special occasion."

"You're welcome." He's acting like he didn't hear my ribbing about the lab coat. "Make a wish."

A wish. All of a sudden, I feel an ache in my chest. None of my wishes are happy. None are normal. A normal girl would wish to meet a nice guy, someone who's fun and good-looking. But not me. I wish I could find my parents' killers and the person who sent them, and then find the will and fortitude to kill them.

"Is something the matter?" Eugene asks.

"No," I lie, smoothing out my frown. "It's silly."

"You wish they were here to say happy birthday?" he says softly, switching to Russian.

I nod. It seems pointless to put it into words. As pointless as wishing.

We share a silence during which I stab the first of my eighteen pancakes with my fork and take a bite.

A bite that I have to stop myself from spitting out.

"Eugene . . ." I try to swallow the soggy, half-cooked lump in my mouth. "These are awful."

Oh crap. As soon as I see the hurt look on his face, I realize I could've been more tactful. But seriously, these are the worst-tasting pancakes I've ever had.

"Sorry." He demonstratively puts a pancake into his own mouth and chews it. "I did what the algorithm said." His expression doesn't change; if he can taste the problem, he's not showing it.

"They're called recipes, not algorithms." I move the plate toward him. "And I'm sure it called for butter and salt, things that make food yummy—stuff that's clearly missing from these pancake-esque thingies."

"Potato, potahto . . . Recipes are algorithms." He spears another pancake onto his fork. "And salt and butter are bad for you anyway."

"A lot of good stuff is bad for you." I reach for the cupcake he bought for me and place it on my plate. "And it's funny you brought up potatoes. Did you put that in these pancakes? Because there's this aftertaste—"

"I'm not an idiot, Mira," he says. "If I made potato pancakes, I would call them *draniki.* Do you remember how—"

He doesn't have to finish that question. Of course I remember Mom's draniki. A cross between pancakes and hash browns, they were the most delicious things ever—and a part of my childhood I'll never have again.

I interrupt him by demonstratively blowing out the candle and taking a bite of my cupcake, making that yumminess-signifying, "Mmmmmmm," as I do so.

Eugene smiles at first, but then his face goes dark, an expression so intense and unnatural for him that it frightens me. And considering he's looking over my shoulder, I'm really hoping it's not a huge-ass spider.

"What's that?" He points in that same direction.

"What's what?" Oh shit. Maybe it's one of those giant cockroaches that thrive in this building's garbage disposal system. Or their competitors, the rats.

"That." He stands up and peers at me. "The black-and-blue claw mark on your arm."

I look at my left bicep. Fuck. It seems that Shkillet left a bruise when he grabbed me yesterday.

"It's nothing." I tug my sleeve down—not that it does much good. "Don't worry about it."

"It's not nothing." An even darker look crosses his

face. "How stupid do you think I am?"

"Do you really want me to answer that?" I take a bite of my cupcake and regret it immediately. I know where this is going, and the delicious cupcake begins to taste like cardboard.

"I heard you come in late last night." He sits back down slowly. "You were doing that again. You were consorting with those monsters."

"Calm down." I brush the cupcake crumbs from my fingers.

"How the hell am I supposed to calm down?" He plants his palms on the table, about to shove himself upright again—until I grab his arm. I can feel the tension in him as he yells, "You're coming home with fucking bruises, and you're telling me not to worry about it? It's my job to protect you, and you're on your way to getting yourself killed!"

"Lower your voice, please," I say through clenched teeth. "It's not your fucking job to protect me."

"How can you be so dumb—"

I've had enough. Grabbing the plate from the table, I hurl it toward the stove.

Eugene watches it shatter with utter shock, even though this isn't the first tantrum he's seen me throw in his lifetime. More like the hundredth in the past two years alone.

"Mira, I—" he begins.

"Shut up." I rise to my feet.

"Wait, Mirochka. Seriously, I'm sorry—"

I don't hear the rest because I storm into my

bedroom and slam the door shut behind me. Then I crank up some music and begin throwing clothes into a bag: something casual, a gym outfit, and, on a whim, a nice dress I bought months ago after a spree of poker wins. I also throw in some shoes. I want to make sure I have what I need so I won't have to come back here today—because if I do, I'll have to deal with Eugene's sulking.

"I'm not mad," I say when I open the door again. "I just need to get out of the apartment."

"Don't go, Mirochka—"

"Thank you for the birthday wishes." I sling the bag over my shoulder. "I mean it. It was nice."

"You're welcome." He pinches the bridge of his nose. Eugene knows me well enough to know there's no salvaging this situation right now.

Still, I feel like the biggest asshole as I leave the house.

* * *

Yoga class helps a little. A pretty boy checking out my yoga-pants-clad butt helps a little more. After the gym, I head to my favorite sushi place. That and hot sake make me feel almost like a normal person.

Almost like my birthday is worth celebrating.

Determined to enjoy feeling normal for as long as possible, I take a lengthy walk on the Brighton Beach boardwalk. I try to stay focused on the nice weather, but my thoughts eventually turn to my investigation, as they always do these days.

They said my parents' death was a mob-on-mob hit. Eugene Read the detectives investigating the case, and learned that the police had cut short the investigation as soon as they learned of the Russian mob's involvement. But my dad was never in the Russian mob. He was a scientist, like Eugene. It didn't make any sense until Eugene told me something else that he saw in the mind of the detectives: signs of Pushing.

Pushers are the other side of the coin among people who can enter the Mind Dimension. They're like us—except they control people's minds, instead of reading them. And they hate us just as much as we hate them. It's not a huge surprise those evil fuckers are involved in this somehow, especially given Dad's research into our abilities.

As soon as I learned all this, I knew I had to take the investigation into my own hands. My brother honors our parents' memory by focusing on Dad's research, but I do it differently. I do it by trying to hunt down their murderers, and if it drives my brother crazy, so be it. I'm not a little girl anymore. In fact, as of today, I'm officially an adult—though I haven't felt like a child for a long time.

Determined to get back into my earlier birthday-enjoyment groove, I go to the movies. The one I choose is a romantic comedy, and I enjoy it immensely for the fiction that it is. Those writers make these things so light and fluffy, it's like a fairy tale. In real life—at least in my real life—people are self-destructive, violent liars who will cheat and steal if they can get away with it. Outside of the mob, they put on a façade of civility, but as a Reader, I know what hides behind their polite smiles. In the mob, they don't even try to hide it. The criminals are more honest, in a way. Then again, the depravity of some of the things I Read in Victor's club and other similar places is mind-boggling. I sometimes can't sleep for weeks after getting one of those 'snuff Reads'—

I shake my head. Man, I need to get back some positivity.

To do that, I grab some ice cream before leaving the movie theater. Nothing is more positive than ice cream.

Afterwards, I decide against getting dinner. Instead, I go into the theater bathroom to change into my killer dress, and while I'm at it, I put on some makeup and a pair of high heels. It's time to have some fun and go clubbing. Why the hell not? It's my fucking birthday.

* * *

"Are you Russian?" is what I think the guy tries to say to me over the pounding music of the dance club.

"Da," I yell, nodding to the beat.

"Can I buy you a drink?" he says in Russian. Or I assume that's what he says because I catch the Russian word for drink over the noise, and he also puts his hand to his mouth in that universal drinking gesture. Not to mention, he points at the bar.

I look the guy over. Tall, broad-shouldered, he looks like the kind of guy I would've liked if I'd remained normal. Since I'm trying to be normal tonight, I let him buy me a Grey Goose with Red Bull, my party-all-night drink.

I love these Russian-owned clubs, even if sometimes the owners are in the mob. The vodka selection is always topnotch, the DJs are great at mixing the tracks, the music they mix is more to my taste, and the bartenders never ask for ID. I have a fake one, of course, but I prefer not to be asked. What's more, here they never give you that I-know-that-ID-is-fake-but-hey-now-I'm-off-the-hook-little-girl look.

As I sip my drink, the guy introduces himself and gives me some compliments, but I only hear bits and pieces. Finally, I have to lean in and yell into his ear, "I can barely hear you!"

"Would you like to dance?" He leans down, yelling into my ear, and I can finally hear him.

"Absolutely." I'm about to add his name, but realize that I can't remember it. Talk about embarrassing. I can't ask him now. Of course, I can always Split and check his wallet for an ID, so maybe later I'll do that.

He's a great dancer, with a sense of rhythm that I haven't been lucky enough to run into before. And speaking of lucky, I've lucked out in that he's also just the right amount of grabby. Although, after a song or two, with the buzz from the drink starting to hit my brain, I decide that he's not grabby enough. I take his hands and stick them on my butt. He, smart guy that he is, gets the point, and from here on out, there's a lot more touching. He even goes for some ear-nibbling, which I approve of.

We dance like that for at least ten songs. My legs begin to ache, and my head is spinning. I feel great. I feel as if . . . well, as if it's my fucking birthday.

Another few songs, and I'm grinding against him. He clearly likes it—that or there's a flashlight in his pocket that I hadn't noticed before.

"Do you want to get out of here?" he asks me eventually.

"Sure." I give him one last grind—in case there's any misunderstanding as to where this night is headed. "Let's go to your place."

He's holding my hand as we start making our way through the crowd, and then, suddenly, he stops.

He's staring at the chest of a gargantuan bouncer.

"Leave," the bouncer growls. He must have sixty pounds' worth of lungs alone; I can hear him clearly over all the noise. "She stays."

"What's the problem?" the guy asks.

"You didn't hear me?" The bouncer starts rolling up his sleeves—never a good sign. In a Russian nightclub, could be a deadly sign.

"It's all right," I yell at my guy. "I know this man."

"You're with him?" His lips become a thin line. "Why didn't you tell me you were with someone?"

I shrug, taking his anger as a compliment. I'd love to tell him the truth, but whatever this shit with the bouncer is about, there's no reason to bring a civilian into it. Especially a guy who showed me a good time.

The guy walks away, shaking his head.

"Upstairs," the bouncer barks. "This way." He leads me up the stairs and points to a closed door with a tinted glass window in it. There's no way I can see what's waiting for me inside.

Damn. I shouldn't have left the gun in my car. Oh well, I think, and open the door.

"Hello," Victor says when the bouncer opens the door for me. "We need to talk."

Of all the clubs owned by shady people, I clearly chose the worst one.

And then I realize there's someone else in the room.

A man I didn't expect to see, let alone this soon.

Shkillet, his face black and blue with the injuries I inflicted, gives me a look that says, "You're dead now, bitch."

CHAPTER FIVE

"You have questionable taste in comrades, Victor." I'm not going to let either of them think they've thrown me. Never let them see you sweat—it's a motto I live by.

Shkillet's face reddens, and he reaches for his boot, but stops. "She's trying to disrespect you," he whispers to Victor, loudly enough that I can hear.

"When I want your opinion, Shkillet, I will provide it." Victor rises from his chair as Shkillet's red face turns white. "As for you, my lovely friend—" Victor inclines his head toward me, "—there's a very good reason why he's here."

"And that would be what? You need your toilets licked clean?" I stare at Shkillet, not backing down from the threat I see in his eyes.

"You whore." Shkillet's fingers twitch, likely

itching to get to that knife. I know; I've felt that same hatred myself. Thankfully, he elects to spit on the ground instead of trying to skewer me.

"Spit on my floor again, and you'll be licking it off, Shkillet, understand? Also don't speak again until I say you can." If looks actually could kill, Victor's would've already murdered Shkillet ten times over. "Do I make myself clear?"

Shkillet nods, and I can tell it's killing him to do so.

Victor glares at him. "Say it."

Shkillet exhales. "I'll wait for you to ask me to speak, Victor." It sounds as if the words are being pulled from him.

"Now." Victor tugs his sleeves down. "As I was saying, there is a reason he's here, and it's because an accusation has been made."

"An accusation?" I try not to sound challenging—a task I, admittedly, have trouble with on occasion.

"Our comrade here told me some disturbing things about you." Victor leans against a table, arms crossed. "He claims that you work with the cops as a snitch, or worse, that you're a cop yourself."

"What?" I didn't expect that, and I don't have any clever, or even dumb, comebacks for him. "What are you talking about?"

"He said you'd deny it." Victor picks up a shot glass that's been standing on his desk and downs the contents in one gulp. "But his story is rather persuasive, so I figured we should talk."

This is bad. If Victor really believes this, I'm as

good as dead. I debate Splitting and Reading him to figure out what's what, but decide against it. After yesterday, my Depth is fairly low, even if some was recovered in the twenty-four hours that have passed. Still, if I overuse it, I'll go Inert and be unable to Split for many days.

"I'm not a cop." I start to fold my arms in front of my chest, realize it's a defensive gesture, and run my hands through my hair instead. "That's a ridiculous notion that only that syphilitic excuse for a brain could've come up with—"

"Suka." The Russian insult comes out of Shkillet with a snarl.

"I thought I told you to shut it." Victor points one threatening finger at Shkillet. "It's not that ridiculous, my dear. He says cops—your colleagues—did that to his face."

"Cops didn't do it. I did."

"I wasn't done." Now I'm the recipient of Victor's threatening finger. "What he said is just a piece of the puzzle, you see. After that last game yesterday, I asked around."

"And?" I ask, not liking where this is going.

"And you do have a tendency to . . . How should I put this delicately? To ask some odd questions during pillow talk."

Shkillet sneers, and I try not to blush. It's true that I've slept with a few gangsters. No one too monstrous, mind you, but definitely bad boys. I didn't do it just to get information, though. I was attracted to them—though I'm not sure if that makes it better or worse. Yeah, I did end up asking about explosion experts when a good moment presented itself, and if it just happened to be post-coitus . . . Well, that's when most men seem to let their guard down.

"I'm just interested in certain things." I shrug. "Maybe I'm looking for someone to do a job for me. To settle a score. That doesn't make me a cop."

Victor stares at me. I meet his gaze. I'm determined not to show any weakness. And right now, my knees are feeling pretty weak. I don't know what Victor has up his proverbial sleeve, and I don't know where he's going with this. I do much better when I have all the information.

"There's also the matter of your name. You claim it's Ilona, but we both know that you also go by Mira and Yulia and a bunch of others."

Crap. Where did he get that from? I thought I'd covered my tracks well. Changing my name was actually for my brother's sake, the going theory being that whoever killed Dad, if controlled by a Pusher, would want Eugene dead as well. But I can't exactly tell Victor that.

"I win large sums of money." I think really hard and really quickly, something I've learned to be good at. "Not just from you, but other legal venues as well. You can check with your people in Vegas. Given that, I think it's only natural for me to want to retain some anonymity."

"I can see that. To a point." Victor takes a big bottle of vodka and refills his shot glass. "But you must see how, bundled together, this doesn't look good."

"No, I don't agree." I shift my weight from one foot to another. "I'd make the worst, most conspicuous undercover cop in the history of undercover work. I mean, I'm usually the only woman at those games. I stick out like a sore thumb."

"She has a point there." Victor waves his shot glass in Shkillet's direction. "Even if I'd use a prettier metaphor to describe her."

"Why are you even listening to her?" Shkillet says in frustration. "She'll say anything to get out of here with her head still attached."

"Because something more is going on here." Victor downs the shot he's been holding. "And I find this one rather interesting."

"Then let me make her talk." Shkillet takes his knife out, his hands practically shaking with eagerness. "Two minutes, and she'll admit that she's a cop, just like I say she is."

"We'll talk about you sneaking a weapon into this establishment in a moment." Victor gives him a furious look. "First, I want to point something out to you. *I* ask the questions. I don't need your help. I'm a good judge of people, and I know she's hiding something. But I also think you're not telling everything."

"Oh, he's hiding things from you," I say, deciding to escalate matters.

"Is that so?" Victor raises his eyebrows, as if I can't possibly know what I'm talking about. "What would he dare hide?"

"The fact that it was me who fucked up his face, as I was trying to explain earlier," I say. "And that's just for starters."

"That's a lie." Shkillet's knuckles whiten around the hilt of his knife. "It was the cops."

"Also, he's hiding the fact that he's disrespected you." I ignore Shkillet's denial. "He's said things behind your back."

"Before you go further, my dear *Ilona—*" Victor holds up his hand, "—you should know that I won't treat a baseless accusation like that lightly."

"Baseless accusation, like calling me a cop?" I narrow my eyes at Victor. "How's this? He said he fucked your mistress. Though I think he actually raped her, because what woman in her right—"

"What the fuck are you talking about?" Shkillet growls, but shuts up when he looks at Victor.

I see why. Victor's face darkens, and it's scary to see, especially since it's most likely me, not Shkillet that he's angry at.

Without a word, Victor reaches into his desk, pulls out a gun, and places it on the desk with a loud clink of metal on glass. "I think you didn't understand me when I said I wouldn't take to this sort of shit lightly."

I nod. "I understood. But did he?" I point to Shkillet.

"You're a cop," Shkillet shouts. "And I sure as hell didn't go near Victor's lady."

"Oh really?" I say. "Then how would I know her

name is Vera, if not from you?"

"You're a cop." Shkillet moves the knife from one hand to another, nervously.

"And how about the fact that she has a tattoo on her back of the Madonna holding the baby Jesus? The tattoo with a face you wanted to come all over?" I say. "Do I know that also because I'm a cop? Because you told my 'colleagues' that when they beat you up? How about the claim you made that she has a muscular back with dimples and a mole on her right shoulder? You're trying to say that it was some other fucking rapist who told people that?"

Victor's face is the most frightening thing I've seen in a long time. Shkillet sees it, he sees Victor reach for the gun, and he completely flips out, lunging at me with the knife.

Now I Split—no point in having leftover Depth if I'm dead.

In the Mind Dimension, I walk over to Shkillet so I can Read him to verify his intent. As I suspected, he knows he's a dead man and wants to make sure he takes me down with him.

Fuck. I overdid it with him. I didn't think he'd go for the kamikaze thing. At least he made me look honest, which means Victor will probably not only kill him, but do it slowly. Still, if Shkillet kills me first, his destiny will be only a small consolation for me.

I look at Victor. He's still angry, but confused, too. He didn't expect Shkillet to do what he did either. Like me, he probably didn't think the man had the balls for it.

I look at the path of Shkillet's body and the knife. I try my best to project it another foot, to where my frozen self is. I now know what I have to do.

Somewhat encouraged, I get out of the Mind Dimension.

As soon as my consciousness is back in my body, I begin to twist myself just the right way and step aside, hoping I didn't miscalculate.

Shkillet's knife swooshes through the air an inch from my neck.

I didn't miscalculate, thank God.

Shkillet comes to a dead stop, his beady eyes wide with shock. He can't believe I escaped his attack.

I see a blur of movement so I Split again.

Shit. He recovered too quickly. He's frozen in the process of making a wide swing at me. Unless I do something, he's going to disembowel me with that knife.

I look at Victor. In the few moments that have passed, he's grabbed the gun from his desk. But even if it's my opponent rather than me that Victor intends to shoot, it'll take too long for him to complete that movement, let alone aim the gun and fire it at Shkillet.

Besides, if he did that, there's no telling whether he'd shoot the wrong person—namely, me—given how close I'm standing to Shkillet. I decide against Reading Victor to see who he's going to aim that gun at. I have no Depth to waste on questions where the answer won't help the situation at hand. Instead, I

Split back.

Even before my mind is back in my body, I begin mentally playing out a maneuver that I can best describe as a hula-hoop move. I try to do it over and over, to make sure it's the first and only thing that my body does when it gets the mind back. My body moves in the desired motion, but not fast enough, and I feel a burning pain in my side.

A pain that makes me involuntarily Split again.

Please, God, don't let me see myself dying. I turn to look at my frozen body in the Mind Dimension.

I'm in luck. Even though the hula-hoop move wasn't entirely successful, it did get me far enough out of the knife's path. Shkillet only grazed my side. And now he's off-balance.

I Split and get back to real time with a whirling kick to Shkillet's balls, a move I've done many times since starting my investigation. Nothing stops a man as quickly as a hit in that vulnerable place, and no man has ever deserved it more than Shkillet.

As my foot connects, Shkillet squeals loudly and grabs his damaged family jewels. Remembering Victor's unfinished vodka bottle, I grab it, determined to bring it down on Shkillet's head. But before I can, a shot rings out.

My heart feels like it's going to jump out of my ribcage as the room goes silent.

I automatically Split again and look around. My real body doesn't look like it's been shot. There's some more blood flowing from where Shkillet's knife grazed me, but that's it. When I glance at Victor's gun, I can't tell where he's pointing it because the air around the barrel is filled with smoke.

When I turn toward Shkillet, however, I see that the right side of his skull is flying away, with bits of blood and brain matter frozen in the air. So that's where Victor was aiming. And what's more, there's another bullet frozen midway on its trajectory toward Shkillet's chest.

Exhaling in relief, I decide to spend a few more precious moments of my Depth to Read Victor's intentions. If he's planning to shoot me, I want to know about it, even if there's not much I can do to stop him. Then again, maybe I'll throw that vodka bottle at him—get one last shot in before I go.

Inside Victor's head, I experience rage mixed with awe mixed with confusion. It's impossible to tell what he'll do for sure, so I leave the Mind Dimension and get ready to face whatever is in store for me.

Victor looks at Shkillet's bleeding body, then looks at me, the gun pointing at me for a brief, heart-pounding moment, but then he slowly lowers the weapon.

A bouncer rushes into the room. "What the fuck, boss? Your glass door is not that soundproof. If I heard it outside, anyone on the dance floor could've, too."

"We'll need some private cleaning in here." Victor puts his gun down on the table. "And as for the noise, tell the DJ to make up an excuse about a problem with his equipment. Also tell him to announce a half hour of open bar, starting now."

"Got it." The bouncer exhales and rolls his shoulders as he heads out the door. "That'll work, especially the second part."

"I'm not sure what just happened," Victor says when the bouncer leaves. "What you said about Vera was accurate, and only someone who's seen her naked would know those things. But something doesn't ring true because I have a hard time believing he'd dare." Victor waves toward what's left of Shkillet, and shakes his head. "Still, I did underestimate the little creep tonight. I ought to put on his tombstone: 'Shkillet, the underestimated.'"

"I'd make that 'Shkillet, the underestimated rapist.'" I give the dead body a shove with my foot.

"I don't know about that part." Victor extends his hand for the bottle I'm still holding.

"Believe what you want." I hand him the bottle. "Ask around. He was a rapist."

"But did he do that to Vera?" Victor frowns, pouring himself another shot. "That's what I have trouble with. Wouldn't she have told me?"

"She was probably ashamed. It happens a lot with rape victims. All I can say is, if he didn't, he sure lied about it. Just like he lied about me being a cop."

"And you're not?" Victor gulps down the shot. "You moved like some Spetsnaz soldier when he attacked you. It was—"

"I have good reflexes." I have to get his mind off what he thinks he saw. "That's all. It doesn't make me a cop."

"But it does make you an accessory to this." He

points to Shkillet. "But here's what bothers me. If he lied and didn't fuck her, how'd he know what she had on her back?"

"Well, we can't ask him now." I shrug. "Maybe he was a peeping tom? That's not strange for a rapist."

"Perhaps." He gives me a suspicious stare. "Or maybe you are. Did you see me fuck her yesterday? Did you watch us and use the info to make it look like he disrespected me?"

"You wish. That's one of *your* voyeuristic fantasies. Besides, wouldn't you close the door and have some bouncer guard it if you were fucking?"

Victor sighs and rakes his fingers through his hair. "Talking to you is as frustrating as talking to Nadia. You're too good of a liar—probably helps you during poker."

I shrug and pretend not to know he's talking about his daughter.

"So." Victor exhales. "The fact that he attacked you could mean you're right. Maybe he knew that if he didn't attack you, his death would've been . . . slow."

"You give him too much credit. He's not that smart—only crazy." I twirl my finger next to my temple in a gesture for insanity.

Victor chuckles, but then he stops abruptly and stares at me.

Feeling like I'm under a magnifying glass, I can't help but notice the throbbing in my wound. The adrenaline rush has worn off, and it hurts like a son of a bitch.

"You're bleeding." He frowns.

"It's nothing." I don't want to give him the satisfaction of admitting to weakness. "But thanks for your concern."

"Listen, whatever-your-name-is, I want to continue this conversation someday."

Great. Just what I don't need. I think it, but don't verbalize it.

"In the meantime," he continues, "I'll spread the word that you're under my protection so you won't need to worry about the likes of Shkillet in the future."

I'm at a loss for words. I didn't expect him to say that. That's the third time I'm surprised today. I really should Read people more if I don't want these surprises, but it's tricky because of my limited Depth.

"Here's my card." He hands it to me as if this is a normal business deal. "Call me if you need anything."

I take the card. Then he walks to the door and lets his bouncers in.

"Take her to the hospital," Victor tells the big guy who brought me here earlier. "Put the bill on my tab." He looks at me after the bouncer nods. "I'll be seeing you later, Ilona."

Numb with shock, I let myself be herded through the club. There's no sign of the guy I'd danced with. Oh well. It's not like that would've been anything more than a one-night stand. I'm nothing if not realistic. There's no room in my life for a relationship.

* * *

Patched up and tired as a dog, I take a cab from the hospital to my car.

As I watch the streets whiz by, I have a million thoughts running through my head. They fight with one another, but the one that keeps getting my attention is that I have to get away. Away from Brooklyn, away from gangsters, away from all this shit. I need to let things settle here.

It's a smart idea, but what can I do? Where should I go?

Ideas pop up, then fizzle out. Should I visit Vegas again? No, I'd need a new set of IDs for that, since they're onto me big-time in that town. Monte Carlo is still out of reach; my fake papers aren't good enough for Europe.

As I get home and sneak into my room again, I realize that there is another place I could go. It's closer, and there's less heat for me there, even if it's not that far distance-wise.

By the time I get into bed, I'm on board with my new plan. I'll get a couple of nights of good sleep, get my stitches taken out, patch things up with Eugene, and then grab a bus to Atlantic City.

Has anyone been this excited about a trip to New Jersey before? I don't know, and I don't care. My world becomes all about the softness of my pillow as I fall into a blissful and much-deserved sleep.

FROM THE AUTHOR

Thank you so much for reading *The Time Stopper*. If you'd like to read more about Mira, you can check out *The Thought Readers (Mind Dimensions: Book 1)*. It's told from the point of view of Darren, a young man who meets Mira on her trip to Atlantic City.

If you like epic fantasy, I also have a series called *The Sorcery Code*. You can find it at most retailers.

If you don't mind erotic material and are in the mood for sci-fi romance, you can also check out *The Krinar Chronicles*, my collaboration with Anna Zaires, my wife. You can grab the first volume, *Close Liaisons*, FREE as an ebook at most retailers.

To sign up for my new release email list and learn

more about my works, please visit my website at www.dimazales.com.

Also, if you enjoyed this novelette, I would be very grateful if you helped other readers discover it by leaving a review and mentioning it to your friends and social media connections.

I love to hear from readers, so be sure to:
-Friend me on Facebook:
https://www.facebook.com/DimaZales
-Like my Facebook page:
https://www.facebook.com/AuthorDimaZales
-Follow me on Twitter:
https://twitter.com/AuthorDimaZales
-Follow me on Google+:
https://www.google.com/+DimaZales
-Friend or follow me on Goodreads:
https://www.goodreads.com/DimaZales

CPSIA information can be obtained at www.ICGtesting.com
Printed in the USA
LVOW04s2027190515

439048LV00004B/877/P